First published by Parragon in 2011

Parragon
Queen Street House
4 Queen Street
Bath BA1 1HE, UK

Copyright © 2011 Disney Enterprises, Inc
Visit www.DisneyFairies.com

ISBN 978-1-4454-2790-4

Printed in China

Contents

Bath • New York • Singapore • Hong Kong • Cologne • Delhi
Melbourne • Amsterdam • Johannesburg • Auckland • Shenzhen

Tinker Bell

ADAPTED BY LISA MARSOLI
ILLUSTRATED BY THE DISNEY STORYBOOK ARTISTS

On a chilly winter's night in London, a baby lay peacefully in her crib. As her mobile twirled, the baby let out her very first laugh and – as with all first laughs – a fairy was born!

The laugh floated out of the window and attached itself to a dandelion wisp. It flew above the human world straight towards the Second Star to the Right, and through a burst of light into Never Land!

Queen Clarion approached. "Born of laughter, clothed in cheer, happiness has brought you here. Welcome to Pixie Hollow," she said.

The newcomer flapped her wings. She could fly! Next, other fairies began to place objects in front of the new fairy.

"These objects will help you find your talent," the queen explained.

The new fairy timidly placed her hand on each object, but nothing happened. She was discouraged. But as she passed the hammer, it started to glow. Then it flew straight to her!

"I've never seen one glow that much," said Silvermist.

Vidia fumed. She had one of the strongest and rarest talents in Pixie Hollow, and she wasn't looking for competition.

"Come forward, tinker fairies," called the queen, "and welcome the newest member of your talent guild – Tinker Bell!"

Bobble and Clank, two tinker fairies, took Tinker Bell to Tinkers' Nook. She saw a small courtyard lined with twig-and-leaf cottages. Fairies were fixing and fashioning all kinds of amazing, useful objects.

Clank and Bobble dropped
Tinker Bell off at her own little
house. All the clothes in her
closet were much too big. Luckily,
Tink knew just what to do.

Tinker Bell put on her new dress, tied her hair up, and reported to the workshop.

Soon Fairy Mary – the no-nonsense fairy who ran Tinkers' Nook – arrived.

"So dainty!" Fairy Mary exclaimed as she looked at Tink's hands. "Don't worry, dear, we'll build up those tinker muscles in no time."

Then, after reminding Clank and Bobble to make their deliveries, Fairy Mary was gone.

A little while later, Tink, Clank and Bobble set out to deliver some springtime items to the nature fairies, with help from Cheese the mouse.

Suddenly, the fairies heard a sound behind them. *PITTER-PATTER! PITTER-PATTER!*

"Sprinting Thistles! Aaaaagh!" screamed Clank.

The weeds nearby had come to life and were rushing towards them!

The wagon flew down the path and crashed in the middle of Springtime Square.

Thankfully, the tinkers were unhurt. They began to make their deliveries. There were milkweed-pod satchels for an animal fairy named Fawn, pussy willow brushes for a garden fairy named Rosetta, and rainbow tubes for Iridessa, a water fairy.

A light fairy named Silvermist was there, too. She sprayed water into the air. When Iridessa flew through the droplets, a perfect rainbow was formed. Iridessa rolled it up into a tube.

"I'm going to take it to the mainland," she explained to Tink.

"What's the mainland?" the new fairy asked.

"It's where we're going for spring, to change the seasons," replied Silvermist.

Next, the tinkers stopped at the Flower Meadow. Vidia zipped by, using her whirlwind to pull pollen from the flowers.

"Hi!" said Tinker Bell. "What's your talent?"

"I am a fast-flying fairy," answered Vidia. "I make breezes in summer and blow down leaves in autumn. Fairies of every talent depend on me."

"Tinkers help fairies of every talent, too!" Tink said excitedly.

"I make forces of nature. You make pots and kettles," Vidia pointed out. "It's not like spring depends on you."

"When I go to the mainland, I'll prove just how important we are!" Tink replied.

Tink flew off, grumbling to herself. Soon, however, she was distracted by something shiny down on the beach. She flew closer. It was a coin! Tink began digging. Before long she had found all sorts of treasures. She scooped them up and took them to the workshop.

"You've found Lost Things," explained Clank when Tink arrived.

"They wash up on Never Land from time to time," said Bobble. "Not much good for anything, though."

Fairy Mary whisked Tink's trinkets away. The Queen's Review of the springtime preparations was that night, and there was still a lot to do.

Tink knew this was her chance to prove just how important a tinker's talent really was!

That evening, the Minister of Spring welcomed Queen Clarion to the review ceremony. "When the Everblossom blooms, we will be ready to bring spring to the mainland," he said proudly.

Suddenly, Tinker Bell arrived. "I came up with some fantastic things for tinkers to use when we go to the mainland!" she called.

Before the queen could say anything, Tink pulled out a homemade paint sprayer. But instead of spraying colour, it exploded, making a huge mess!

The queen looked at Tinker Bell kindly. "Tinker fairies don't go to the mainland," she said. "All the springtime work is done by the nature fairies. I'm sorry."

Tink returned to the workshop. "Being a tinker stinks," she grumbled.
"Excuse me?" replied Fairy Mary.
"Why don't we get to go to the mainland?" Tink asked.
"The day you can magically make the flowers grow or capture the rays of the sun, you can go. Until then, your work is here," said Fairy Mary impatiently.
Suddenly, Tink smiled slyly. She had an idea.

The next morning, Tink found her friends at the Pixie Dust Well.

"If you could teach me your talents, maybe the queen would let me go to the mainland," Tink said.

No fairy had ever changed his or her talent! Reluctantly, Tink's friends agreed to help. Silvermist was first. The water fairy showed Tink how to place a dewdrop on a spiderweb.

But each time Tink tried, the dewdrop burst.

Next, Iridessa demonstrated how to give fireflies their glow. She captured light in a bucket and scattered it. Dozens of fireflies flew through it and lit up. But when Tink tried, the light wouldn't stick to her fingers. She threw the bucket in frustration. The light spilled in every direction. Now she was glowing, too!

The fireflies swarmed around her – they thought she was the most beautiful thing they had ever seen!

Fawn had Tink's animal-fairy lesson all planned. "We're teaching baby birds how to fly," she announced.

Fawn showed Tink what to do.

Unfortunately, Tink's bird was terrified. He didn't want to go anywhere.

31

Tink saw a majestic bird flying overhead. *Maybe he can help!* she thought. She waved her hand and tried to get the bird's attention. The scout fairies looked to see what was going on.

"Hawk! Hawk!" they yelled, sounding their warning horns.

Tink spotted a tree with a knothole and rushed straight for it.

The hole was already occupied – by Vidia.

CRACK! The hawk broke through the bark with his beak. The two fairies had to get out of there – fast! They jumped down a hole into a long, dark tunnel.

When Vidia reached the end of the tunnel, she could see the hawk on a nearby branch. She stopped in the nick of time – but Tink accidentally slammed into her. Vidia went shooting out of the tree. The hawk opened his beak, ready to strike. Fairies pelted him with berries, rocks and twigs. Luckily, the bird flew away.

"Let me help you," Tink said to Vidia.

"I'm fine!" snapped Vidia.

"I was only trying to help," Tink explained. She felt awful.

A little while later, Tinker Bell sat on the beach.

"At this rate, I should get to the mainland right about, oh, never!"

Tink angrily threw a pebble into the bushes and heard a *CLUNK!*

She went to investigate and found a beautiful porcelain box.

When her friends found her, Tinker Bell was busy putting all the gears and screws and springs back inside the box. The final touch was attaching a ballerina to the lid. Tinker Bell gave the dancer a spin and, to her delight, the box played music!

"Do you even realize what you're doing?" asked Rosetta. "Fixing stuff like this – that's what tinkering is!"

"Who cares about going to the mainland, anyway?" Silvermist added.

But Tink still wanted to go.

Tink went to see the only fairy she thought might be able to help. But Vidia was not in the mood for visitors – especially Tinker Bell.

"You're my last hope,"pleaded Tink. "Rosetta won't even try to teach me to be a garden fairy."

That gave Vidia an evil idea. She suggested that Tinker Bell capture the Sprinting Thistles to prove that she would be a good garden fairy.

Tink knew that Vidia's plan was her last chance to go to the mainland. She set to work building a corral.

"Hi-yah! Go! Go!" Tinker Bell cried as she rode out into Needlepoint Meadow atop Cheese. She used two twigs to herd some Thistles into the corral.

"It's working!" Tink cried joyfully. But as she headed back to the meadow, Vidia quietly blew open the corral gate. The Thistles ran away.

Soon other Thistles popped up to join the ones that had escaped. It was a stampede! The Thistles headed toward Springtime Square, trampling over the carefully organized springtime supplies.

Everything was destroyed. And it was all Tinker Bell's fault.

"There isn't a garden fairy alive who can control those weeds!" Rosetta exclaimed.

"This has all gone too far," declared Silvermist.

Just then, Queen Clarion appeared. "By the Second Star! All the preparations for spring..."

"I'm sorry," Tinker Bell whispered as she took to the sky.

A little while later, Tink went to the Pixie Dust Well. She told Terence she was leaving Pixie Hollow. He kindly gave her a double scoop of the glittering dust.

"Thanks, Terence," said Tink.

Terence was surprised she knew his name. "I'm just a dust-keeper," he said, "not exactly seen as the most important fairy in Pixie Hollow."

"You're probably the most important one there is!" Tink argued. "You should be proud!"

"I am," Terence replied.

Tink could tell that Terence knew she wasn't proud of *her* talent.

Tink stopped in to visit the workshop one last time. She did love to tinker – even though her contraptions never worked.

Just then, she noticed that Cheese was sniffing something. It was the pile of trinkets she had found on the beach.

"Lost Things... that's it!" she cried. She went to her worktable and started to tinker.

That night, Queen Clarion gathered all the fairies. She explained that spring would not arrive that year, since there wasn't time to replace what had been ruined.

"Wait!" Tinker Bell cried, "I know how we can fix everything!"

She demonstrated her paint sprayer, which she had fixed so that it worked perfectly. Tink had also designed speedy machines to fix the things the Thistles had trampled.

Vidia was furious. "Corral the Thistles..." she muttered. "I should have told you to go after the hawk!"

Queen Clarion overheard this. She looked sharply at Vidia. "I think your fast-flying talent is well suited to chasing down each and every one of the Thistles," the queen said sternly.

Vidia flew away. All of a sudden, she had a lot of work to do.

The queen turned to Tinker Bell. "Are you sure you can do this?" she asked.

"I'm a tinker, and tinkers fix things," Tink replied confidently. "But I can't do it alone!"

Clank, Bobble and all the fairies offered to help. Soon the square was filled with piles and piles of useful objects.

Tink showed a group of fairies how to assemble a machine to make berry paint. As soon as all the pieces of the machine were put together, the berries were crushed, and dozens of buckets were filled to the brim with paint.

Next, Tink used a glove and a harmonica to make a vacuum. The fairies could use it to collect hundreds of seeds at a time.

Everywhere she looked, Tinker Bell could see baskets and buckets of springtime supplies. Her plan was working!

Early the next morning, Queen Clarion and the ministers of the seasons flew to the square. They couldn't believe their eyes – there were more springtime supplies than they had ever seen!

As the sun began to rise, the Everblossom opened. It was time to take spring to the mainland! The fairies cheered.

"Can't Tink come with us?" Silvermist asked.

"It's okay," Tink protested. "My work is here."

Fairy Mary gave a little whistle, and Clank appeared with the music box.

"Actually, I ran across this myself many seasons ago," said Fairy Mary. "Didn't have a clue how to fix it. But you did, Tinker Bell. And I'd imagine there's someone out there who's missing this. Perhaps a certain tinker fairy has a job to do after all...on the *mainland*."

Tink and the other fairies flew toward London. When they arrived, everything was cold and the landscape was grey.

The fairies spread out across the city. A light fairy melted the frost on a tree branch. A water fairy sprinkled pixie dust on a frozen pond to thaw the ice. The animal fairies gently woke the hibernating creatures tucked inside the trees. Soon flowers bloomed and baby birds took flight. Tink was amazed by the magic her friends created!

Now it was time for Tinker Bell to make her special delivery. She sprinkled some of the extra pixie dust Terence had given her on the music box, to make it fly. As Tink passed a bedroom window, both she and the music box began to glow. Tink knew that the owner of the music box must live there.

Tink tapped on the glass and ducked out of sight. In a few moments, a little girl named Wendy Darling poked her head out the window. Wendy's face filled with happiness. She took a small key from a chain around her neck and turned it in a slot. The music box began to play!

The fairies' work was done. It was time for them to return to Never Land.

From then on, Tink used her rare talent to make the lives of everyone in Pixie Hollow just a little bit better. She was proud to be a tinker fairy!

The End

Tinkerbell
and the Lost Treasure

ADAPTED BY LISA MARSOLI
ILLUSTRATED BY THE DISNEY STORYBOOK ARTISTS

Summer was over. It was time for the fairies of Pixie Hollow to bring the beautiful season of autumn to the mainland! Unseen by the humans below, they burst through the clouds and began working their magic.

Soon the whole world was full of the warm colours of autumn. The fairies headed for the Second Star to the Right to make their journey home.

Back in Pixie Hollow, other fairies were collecting pixie dust from the Pixie Dust Tree. Pixie dust made it possible for all fairies to do their special kinds of magic.

When the buzzer signaling the end of the workday sounded, Terence bid his fellow dust-keepers goodbye. As usual, he was off to help his best friend, Tinker Bell, with her latest invention.

Terence found Tinker Bell at the stream putting the finishing touches on her new boat, the Pixie Dust Express. Soon she was ready for a test run. She launched the gourd boat into the water and Terence got into a leaf boat and paddled up beside her.

"Don't worry. I'll be right next to you," he said. "Let'er rip!"

Tink pulled the rip cord and the Pixie Dust Express zoomed away.

"Whoa!" cried Terence as a huge spray of water from Tink's boat sank his.

Tink sped along, pulling various levers. Suddenly, wings, skis and a waterwheel popped out, making her boat move forwards even faster.

"Uh-oh," Tink said as she spotted some rocks up ahead. The boat's skis snapped off, but her craft cruised ashore and kept on going – right towards a tree! The Pixie Dust Express shot up the tree's trunk, coming to rest on the tippy-top, then fell back to the ground.

"Are you okay?" asked Terence.

"I'm good. Thanks," Tink assured him.

"Wow, I'm impressed," Terence said as he helpfully gathered the bits and pieces of her boat. "You're really handling this well."

But Tink couldn't hold her frustration in for long. "Aaargh!" she cried. "I can't believe the boat broke!"

"Ah, it just needs a little tinkering," Terence said breezily. His cheerful attitude had Tinker Bell feeling better in no time.

Suddenly, a fairy arrived with a message. Queen Clarion wanted to see Tinker Bell right away! Tink nervously hurried to the royal chambers, where Queen Clarion, the Minister of Autumn and Fairy Mary were waiting for her.

"Since long, long ago," the minister began solemnly, "fairies have celebrated the end of autumn with revelry – and this particular autumn coincides with a blue harvest moon. A new sceptre must be created to celebrate the occasion." He led Tinker Bell to a hall filled with stunning sceptres. "This year, it is the turn of the tinker fairies."

"And Fairy Mary has recommended you," Queen Clarion declared.

67

Tinker Bell gasped in disbelief.

"At the top of the sceptre you will place a moonstone," the minister continued. He directed everyone's attention to an ancient tapestry hanging on the wall. "When the blue moon is at its peak, its rays will pass through the gem, creating blue pixie dust. The blue pixie dust restores the Pixie Dust Tree."

That night, Terence paid Tink a visit. She told him all about being chosen to create the new autumn sceptre.

"The blue moon only rises in Pixie Hollow every eight years," Terence explained. "The trajectory of the light beams have got to match the curvature of the moonstone at a ninety-degree angle so the light can transmute into pixie dust."

Tink was impressed with Terence's knowledge. When he volunteered to be her assistant, she was all for it!

Day after day, Tink tried out different designs for the sceptre. And day after day,
Terence was there with food, advice and a cheerful willingness to do any job that
Tinker Bell wanted him to do. She couldn't have asked for a more helpful assistant.

As time wore on, though, Tink began to find Terence a bit too helpful. His broom scratched annoyingly on the floor when he swept. He got in her way when she was working. He sometimes stoked the fire so much that the room filled with smoke. Still, she tried to be patient.

Finally, the day came for Tink to finish her creation.

"Steady," said Terence as Tink removed the moonstone from its case.

"I know," replied Tink. "Shhh."

With Terence hovering over her, Tink maneuvered the moonstone closer to the sceptre, but then a piece broke off the setting.

"Looks like you need some sort of sharp thingy," said Terence as Tink tried to repair it.

As he headed out the door to find a tool to do the job, Tink called, "Take your time!"

Once she was alone, Tink was able to concentrate and repair the setting. She placed the moonstone at the top of the sceptre.

Just then, Terence arrived, proudly rolling in a compass he had found at the cove.

"It's your sharp thingy," he announced.

Tink was annoyed. The compass was round – the exact opposite of sharp!

"Would you please get this thing out of here?" she said. She bumped the compass with her hip and it rolled across the room. *WHACK!* The compass hit the sceptre, causing the moonstone to pop out. Then the compass began to spin, finally tipping over and landing on the sceptre.

Tink's beautiful creation shattered instantly.

Tink quickly grabbed the moonstone. "Out!" she yelled at Terence. "You brought this stupid thing here. This is your fault."

Terence was stunned. "Fine! Last time I try to help you!" he yelled back.

Tink set the moonstone down on a cushion and began to pace. She didn't know how she could fix the sceptre in time. In frustration, she kicked the compass with all her might. The cover popped open – and crushed the moonstone!

"No!" Tinker Bell said with a gasp.

That night, after failing to repair the moonstone, Tink desperately tried to figure out what to do next. Her friends Clank and Bobble stopped by.

"Came to see if you wanted to join us for Fairy-Tale Theatre," said Clank.

"I really don't have time," Tink answered nervously.

"Not to worry," Bobble told her. "We'll tell Fairy Mary you couldn't make it."

Suddenly, Tinker Bell realized that Fairy Mary might know where to find another moonstone.

So Tink went to the Fairy-Tale Theatre – but she just couldn't tell Fairy Mary she had broken the moonstone. The show began. A fairy named Lyria appeared.

"'Twas a distant time ago when a pirate ship arrived in Never Land," she began. "The pirates searched until they found a fairy, and forced her to lead them to the enchanted Mirror of Incanta. Forged by fairy magic in ages past, the mirror had the power to grant three wishes."

Next, Lyria told how the pirates made only two wishes before being shipwrecked and losing the mirror forever.

Back at home, Tink quickly drew a map of the lost island, consulted the compass and began to pack some supplies.

"How am I going to carry all this?" she wondered.

Still, she kept packing. "Not enough," she decided as she checked her bag of pixie dust. But Tink wasn't worried. She'd figure out a way to get more.

But the next morning, Tink couldn't talk anyone into giving her more pixie dust. Not knowing where else to turn, she went to Terence and bluntly told him what she needed.

"That's why you're here?" Terence asked. He had been expecting an apology for the way Tink had yelled at him. "Why do you need more dust?"

"A true friend wouldn't ask," said Tink angrily.

"A true friend wouldn't ask me to break the rules!" Terence replied.

"Then I guess we're not true friends," shot back Tink.

"I guess we're not," replied Terence.

Even though Tink didn't think she had enough pixie dust for her journey, she stubbornly moved ahead with her plan. First, she designed and built a vehicle that could carry her and all of her supplies to the lost island. She made what looked like a hot-air balloon from a gourd, a bunch of cotton balls and an array of pots and pans – all in less than a day!

She dressed in her adventurer's outfit and, at dusk, she sprinkled the balloon with pixie dust and lifted off with the moonstone fragments safely tucked in her bag.

"So long, Pixie Hollow!" Tinker Bell called as she rose higher and higher into the sky. "I'll be back soon."

As night fell, Tinker Bell went to have a snack – and discovered an empty supply bag and a very full firefly! She lifted her visitor out of the bag. "Shoo! Go find your friends," she ordered. "I'm on a very important mission."

Tink tried to get rid of the firefly by hurling a stick for him to fetch, but he soon returned. The stick caught on her bag of pixie dust and flung it out of the balloon!

"That does it!" Tink declared to the firefly after she had rescued the bag. "Out!"

The firefly pretended to walk the plank, then jumped off the side of the balloon.

Confident that the troublesome stowaway was gone for good, Tinker Bell turned her attention to her map. The problem was, it was so dark she couldn't see a thing. Suddenly, the map was illuminated by a gentle glow. It was the little firefly!

"Oh, all right," Tink said, giving in. "You can stay. For now. I'm Tinker Bell. What's your name?"

The insect glowed brighter. "Blinky? Flicker? Flash? Beam? Flare?" Tink guessed. Then it came to her. "Oh, Blaze."

In the morning, when a fogbank cleared, they discovered they were stuck in a tree.

"This must be the lost island," Tink decided as she looked around. "And there it is! The stone arch from the story. You stay here and guard the balloon. I'll be right back."

Tink jubilantly flew towards the stone arch. But when she got closer, she saw that it was just the entwined branches of two trees.

Meanwhile, the balloon was starting to drift away! Blaze tried to warn Tink, but she was distracted. By the time he got her attention, the balloon was gone.

"My compass!" yelled Tink. "My supplies! My pixie dust! Why didn't you warn me?"

The pair raced off to find the balloon. Before they could get very far, though, Tink collided with a tree, and everything went black. Blaze sent out a distress call, and within minutes bugs arrived carrying food and water for the injured fairy.

Tink immediately felt better and asked the bugs to lead her to the stone arch. She tried to fly after them, but she couldn't lift off.

"I'm out of dust," she realized. "Guess I'll be walking from here."

As they made their way to the arch, Tink stumbled upon her compass where it had fallen from the balloon. She never would have found it if it weren't for her new little friends.

Tink suddenly realized how much she missed her old friend Terence.

Back in Pixie Hollow, Terence missed Tink, too. That night, he shared his dilemma with a wise old owl. "Tink is my best friend. We should just forgive each other," Terence admitted. "Someone just needs to take the first step."

"Who?" asked the owl.

"I think it should be Tink," Terence said. "She shouldn't have treated me that way."

"Who?" the owl repeated.

It seemed to Terence that the owl was trying to make a point. "Me!" he said suddenly.

Terence flew straight to Tink's house and knocked on the door. There was no answer. "Anyone home?" Terence called as he stepped inside. He felt something crunch under his feet.

"The moonstone!" he gasped.

Investigating further, he discovered the diagram of Tink's balloon and the supply list for her trip. Terence knew that wherever his friend was, she could use some help!

- Pack food
- Pixie dust ?
- Warm Cloth
- Fly nor
- Fin

Back in the forest, Tink and Blaze had reached the next destination in Lyria's rhyme: the old "toll" bridge. But Tink found out that the "toll bridge" was really a "troll bridge", and the trolls weren't cooperating.

"Beat it before we grind your bones to make our bed," said the small troll.

"Make our bread," corrected the tall troll. The small troll got angry, and soon the two were having a heated argument.

They were so busy squabbling that they didn't even notice when Tink and Blaze tiptoed over the bridge!

The two explorers continued across the island and into scrub land. Finally, they emerged from the scrub land onto a beautiful beach. Tink was overjoyed. She had found the pirates' shipwreck!

"Okay, Blaze, this is it! We've got to find that mirror and fix the moonstone. Let's go!"

Nervously, Tink and Blaze ventured into the cold, damp ship. It creaked and moaned as if it were alive – and unhappy at being disturbed.

Tink shivered. "Why couldn't the mirror be in a bunny-filled meadow?" she wondered.

Suddenly, Tink felt something brush past them. Startled, she cried, "Who's that? Who's there?"

Despite their rising fear, the pair continued on to the captain's quarters. "Look, Blaze," said Tink. There, illuminated by a shaft of light, was a bag. Did it hold the gems and gold that Lyria had spoken of? Tinker Bell pulled out the compass needle and hurled it at the bag.

RIIIP! Lost fairy treasure spilled out into a heap on the floor.

Tink reached into the treasure, feeling around and pulled out – the mirror!

She laid the fragments of the moonstone in front of the mirror, then took a deep breath. "I've only got one shot at this," she told herself.

"I wish..." she began, but she was distracted by Blaze's buzzing near her ear. She tried again.

"I wish..." Blaze continued his racket. *BZZZZZ!*

"Blaze, I wish you'd be quiet for one minute!" Tinker Bell shouted.

The buzzing stopped. Tinker Bell gasped. "No, that one didn't count!" she wailed. Her one chance to fix the moonstone was gone.

As one of her tears fell onto the mirror, Terence's face appeared in the reflection.

"Terence!" Tink exclaimed. "I am so sorry."

"I forgive you," replied Terence, "but why didn't you tell me about the moonstone?"

"I didn't think I needed any help," Tink explained. "I was wrong. I wish you were here with me."

"I am with you," said Terence. He was standing right behind her! Tinker Bell ran to her friend. They were so happy to see each other!

"How did you..." Tink began.

"I flew all night and all day over the sea," Terence explained. "And just when I was going to run out of dust, I stumbled into that flying machine of yours. I only had a pinch of dust left. It got me all the way here."

"But where did you even find the dust to make it this far?" Tink asked.

"I...uh...'borrowed' a little extra," Terence admitted.

Tink couldn't believe Terence had broken the rules for her!

Just then, the friends' joyful reunion was interrupted. A vicious pack of rats had come to make a meal of the fairies!

Tink and Terence grabbed the mirror and ran. Blaze tried to distract the rodents by darting and dipping overhead. But it was no use. Terence and Tink were soon surrounded. Thinking quickly, Terence grabbed Tink and swung across the room. *CRASH!* The pair landed on a stack of plates, then rode one through the air like a flying saucer. Suddenly, Terence spotted a loose board in the floor.

"There's our way out," he told Tink. While she tried to pry the board open, Terence held off the rats by brandishing the compass needle like a sword. But when he lost his weapon, the rats began to close in!

Suddenly, the shadow of a hideous monster appeared on the wall! It growled ferociously, sending the rats scurrying away. Tink and Blaze cheered. They had made the "creature" with Blaze's light – and its growls by using Tink's hat as a megaphone!

"C'mere, you vicious monster!" said Tink, giving the firefly a playful rub on the head.

Terence led Tink and Blaze back to the balloon. Luckily, there was just enough pixie dust left in Tink's bag to allow them to lift off.

"I don't know if it will help, but I brought this," said Terence. He handed Tink the shattered sceptre.

"Hey, I've got an idea," Tink announced to Terence. "Would you help me?"

Together, they worked through the night to repair the broken sceptre as the blue moon rose higher in the sky.

Back in Pixie Hollow, the revelry was already under way. But where, Fairy Mary wondered, was Tinker Bell? Suddenly, Tink and Terence swept in, waving and smiling from Tink's balloon. Queen Clarion was impressed. "Now, that's an entrance!" she exclaimed.

Tink walked over and kneeled in front of the queen. "Your Highness," she said with great ceremony.

"Where is the sceptre?" Queen Clarion asked.

"Uh... there were... complications," Tinker Bell replied. "But it's ready now."

Tink removed the leaf covering – and everyone gasped. Her creation was fashioned from the broken bits of the sceptre, the bent mirror frame and fragments of the moonstone. It was beautiful – and wildly unusual.

"Please work, please work, please work," Tinker Bell whispered as the rays from the blue moon began to touch the sceptre.

WHOOSH! The moonbeams reflected everywhere and streaked above the crowd, raining down rare blue pixie dust. At first a flurry, then a shower, then a blizzard, the dust swirled in the air before settling in drifts on the ground.

"Your Majesty!" the Minister of Autumn cried jubilantly. "I've never seen this much blue pixie dust before!"

Fairy Mary agreed. "It's at least a million smidges. Maybe more."

Tinker Bell's fairy friends Silvermist, Fawn, Iridessa and Rosetta were amazed.

"Only Tinker Bell," Iridessa said affectionately.

"Fairies of Pixie Hollow," Queen Clarion said. "Tonight, I believe, is our finest revelry ever, thanks to one very special fairy – Tinker Bell."

Tink pulled Terence close to her and tried to get the queen's attention. "And her friend Terence," added Queen Clarion. Then Blaze flew between Tink and Terence. The queen continued, "And her new friend..."

"Blaze," Tink said.

All the fairies cheered and applauded. The Minister of Autumn handed Tink the sceptre. "All right, everyone, to the Pixie Dust Tree," he announced as Tinker Bell led the procession.

And so that night passed into fairy legend, a story that Lyria would tell for generations to come. But it wasn't a story about the biggest blue pixie dust fall ever. It was a tale of something far more important:

The greatest treasures are not gold,
Nor jewels, nor works of art.
They cannot be held in your hands.
They're held within your heart.
Worldly things will fade away
And seasons come and go,
But the treasure of true friendship
Will never lose its glow.

The End

Disney fairies

Tinkerbell
and the Great Fairy Rescue

ADAPTED BY LISA MARSOLI
ILLUSTRATED BY THE DISNEY STORYBOOK ARTISTS

Tinker Bell and her fairy friends from Pixie Hollow were on their way to bring summer to the mainland. Summer was the busiest of all the four seasons – which meant the fairies would be away from home for months instead of days.

Tinker Bell was so excited! She had heard that the fairy camp where they'd be staying was an amazing place.

Once Tink and the others arrived, the nature fairies got right to work. Vidia, a fast-flying fairy, made the summer grasses sway. Iridessa, a light fairy, bathed flowers in sunshine. Rosetta, a garden fairy, helped bees find their way to the flowers' sweet nectar. Fawn, an animal fairy, greeted birds while Silvermist, a water fairy, frolicked with pollywogs.

Meanwhile, Tink landed in a peaceful clearing.

"Where is everyone else?" she asked Terence, a dust-keeper fairy.

Terence pulled back a tangle of leaves beneath a huge oak tree, revealing the bustling fairy camp.

Tink couldn't wait to get right to work.

"Don't worry, you'll find something to fix," Terence told her. Then he flew off to make pixie dust deliveries.

Just then, a loud *CRACK!* went through the fairy camp!

Fawn was startled and knocked over some paint she was using to decorate butterfly wings. Tinker Bell was very curious about what had caused the loud noise. She flew off to find out.

It was a car! Tinker Bell had never seen one before. Tink followed, and watched as the car stopped at an old house in the country.

Then she saw a little girl, her father, and their cat get out.

"Could we have a tea party in the meadow? Please?" Lizzy, the little girl, pleaded.

"Not today," her father, Dr Griffiths, said wearily. "I have quite a bit of work to do."

117

After the three had gone inside, Tink flew under the car to examine it. Suddenly, Vidia appeared. "You shouldn't be this close to the house!" she scolded.

But Tinker Bell was already poking around the engine. She found an interesting-looking lever and turned it. Outside the car, Vidia got showered with water!

Vidia was furious! Tink knew fairies couldn't fly with wet wings!

Moments later, Lizzy and her father returned to the car – and the fairies froze in fright. Luckily, the humans were busy examining a strange-looking butterfly.

"I guess that's just the way the fairies decided to paint it," Lizzy said.

"Fairies do not paint butterfly wings, because fairies are not real," Dr Griffiths insisted as he captured the creature with a net.

Once the humans left, Tink and Vidia went exploring. They stumbled upon a tiny house in the middle of a clearing.

"Tinker Bell, we're not supposed to go near human houses!" warned Vidia.

"Human houses are a lot bigger," Tink replied. She went inside and looked around, delighted by the tiny furnishings. "It's perfectly safe."

"Oh, really?" asked Vidia. She stepped outside and whipped up a gust of wind that slammed the door shut. Tink didn't mind. She was having fun exploring.

Suddenly, Vidia saw Lizzy approaching in the distance. She pulled on the door to let Tink out – but it was jammed shut!

Tinker Bell saw Lizzy's huge eye staring at her through the window. It was terrifying! Lizzy snatched up the fairy house and raced back home. Vidia followed at a safe distance.

Dr Griffiths was busy studying the butterfly he had captured earlier.

"Now, dear," Dr Griffiths said. "What did you want me to see?"

"Um, never mind..." Lizzy answered. She worried that her father might try to study the fairy the way he was studying the butterfly.

Up in her room, Lizzy took the roof off the fairy house, and *ZIP!* Tinker Bell darted out.
Vidia watched through the window as Mr Twitches pounced. Tinker Bell was in more danger than Vidia had thought!
Lizzy scooped Tinker Bell out of the way and put her in a birdcage for safekeeping. "Bad cat! No, no, no!" cried Lizzy.

Vidia raced back to the fairy camp to get help, but a storm had begun.
"We can't fly in the rain," Fawn reminded her. "And the meadow's already flooded!"
Clank and Bobble had the answer: They would build a boat to take them to save
Tinker Bell!

Back at the house, Lizzy let Tinker Bell out of the cage and showed off her collection of fairy artwork. But as Lizzy described what was going on in each picture, Tink realized that the little girl had her fairy facts all wrong!

Tink interrupted, but all Lizzy heard was a jingling sound. "So that's how fairies speak!" she exclaimed.

Tink went over to the fairy house and started repairing the door.

"Why, you're quite the little tinker, aren't you?" asked Lizzy.

Tink pointed to herself, then rang the house's fairy bell.

"Tinker Bell!" Lizzy cried. "What a lovely name!"

Just then, Dr Griffiths came upstairs to deal with some leaks in the old house's ceilings.

"Lizzy," he said, "it sounds like you're talking to... a fairy?"

Tinker Bell hid while Lizzy quickly held up a fairy drawing. "Oh, yes, but she's make-believe," the little girl replied.

"Quite right," her father said. "I would like to see you spending less time in the fantasy world and more time in the real world. This summer you have an excellent opportunity to learn all sorts of wonderful things. Here is a blank field journal. I'm sure you'll be able to fill it with your own scientific research."

Satisfied, her father went back to his task.

Tinker Bell came out of hiding. She was ready to go home, but a rainstorm had begun!

"You can stay with me until it stops," suggested Lizzy. "You can teach me more about fairies!"

Tinker Bell had an idea. She gathered together some art supplies, then opened the blank field journal.

Lizzy asked her questions about being a fairy, and Tinker Bell acted out the answers.

Soon Tink and Lizzy had filled the journal!

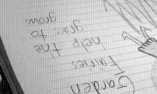

Meanwhile, Tinker Bell's friends were having a rough voyage in their homemade boat. In fact, they were headed straight for a waterfall!

After a wild ride, the boat crashed on the shore. The fairies were safe – but their boat was in pieces. "I guess our sailing days are over," said Bobble.

Now that Lizzy's fairy field journal was complete and the rain was slowing down, it was time for Tink to go find her friends. Tinker Bell was sad about leaving, but excited to get back to the fairy camp.

"Goodbye, Tinker Bell," Lizzy said. "I'll never forget you."

But when Tinker Bell flew past the office window, she saw Lizzy inside. It was obvious the little girl wanted her father to look at her journal – but he was too busy trying to fix all the leaks in the house. Tink realized she couldn't leave just yet. She had to find a way to help Lizzy and her father spend more time together.

Lizzy went back to her room, feeling sad. Suddenly, Tink appeared!
"You came back!" Lizzy exclaimed. She was overjoyed to see her new friend again!

Meanwhile, the other fairies were on foot, continuing their mission to find Tink. Vidia finally spotted the road that led to Lizzy's house. Everyone crossed the road safely except Vidia. She got stuck in the mud! Silvermist, Fawn, Rosetta and Iridessa grabbed on to Vidia and pulled – but they couldn't budge her. Then, suddenly, the fairies saw headlights coming towards them in the rain!

Iridessa held up her hand and bounced the headlight beams back towards the car. The driver stopped and got out. "Is somebody out there?" he asked.

The fairies reached out for his shoelace and held on tight. When the driver turned to leave, he pulled them all out of the mud!

After a fun evening of playing with Tink, and a yummy tea party, Lizzy fell asleep. Tink peeked into the hallway and saw Dr Griffiths give up and head to bed himself as even more drips fell from the ceiling.

That gave Tinker Bell an idea. If she could help Dr Griffiths with the house repairs, he would have more time to spend with Lizzy!

Tinker Bell found a hole in the ceiling and flew up into the attic. The musty old place was filled with crates and boxes – and leaks!

She searched the attic until she had all the parts she needed. In no time at all, she had invented a system to take the water from the leaks and send it back outside.

Tinker Bell flew down into the office to make sure her repairs had worked. She couldn't help noticing the butterfly fluttering in a jar on the desk. It made Tink feel terrible to see the poor creature trapped and helpless.

By the time Tink was done taking care of the leaks, it was morning.

Dr Griffiths came by to check on his daughter. "All the leaks seem to have stopped," he told her. "It's as if they mended themselves."

When Dr Griffiths left the room, Tink picked up the field journal. She encouraged Lizzy to take it to her father.

"I *would* like to show him this," Lizzy said. "He has so much to learn about fairies."

But when Lizzy got downstairs, her father was very upset. "The butterfly is gone," he announced. "I was going to present it at the museum tonight. I didn't let it go, and since there is no one else in this house, it must have been you."

"I didn't," replied Lizzy. "It must have been..."

Tinker Bell started towards the office, but Lizzy waved her away.

"It must have been who?" Dr Griffiths asked.

"I could tell you, Father," Lizzy declared, "but you wouldn't believe me."

"Very well," Dr Griffiths said, "off to your room. I'm very disappointed in you."

In the woods nearby, Tinker Bell's friends made their way silently through the rain.

"I was just thinking, if Tink were here," said Silvermist, "how *not* quiet it would be right now. I really miss her."

"Tinker Bell getting trapped is all my fault," Vidia admitted. "I'm so sorry."

To Vidia's surprise, the other fairies weren't upset with her.

"Tinker Bell can get into plenty of trouble by herself," Rosetta declared.

The fairies joined hands and vowed to work together to save Tink.

142

Meanwhile, Tinker Bell was trying to make Lizzy feel better.

"I wish I were a fairy just like you," Lizzy told Tink. "Then I could fly around with the other fairies all the time."

Tink knew how to make Lizzy's wish come true: pixie dust!

While Lizzy was being a pretend fairy upstairs, lots of real fairies were slipping into the kitchen downstairs to rescue Tink! They didn't get very far, though. Mr Twitches was blocking their way!

Vidia had an idea. She shot a stream of pixie dust at a plate, which began to hover in the air. The others joined in, sprinkling the magic dust on dishes and silverware. Now the fairies hurried across their flying bridge to reach the stairs – but Mr Twitches was right behind them.

"You know where Tink is," Rosetta told Vidia. "You go. We'll take care of the cat."

At the same time, Dr Griffiths could hear strange noises coming from Lizzy's room.

"What's going on in here?" he demanded. "Look at this room! How did you get footprints on the ceiling? The truth this time."

"Well, I..." began Lizzy. "I was flying. My fairy showed me how."

"You've got to stop this nonsense!" insisted Dr Griffiths.

Just then, Vidia sneaked into the room, but he didn't see her.

"You will never convince me that fairies exist!" he added.

Tinker Bell couldn't stand it any longer. She flew out of hiding and hovered directly in front of his face!

"It can't be!" Lizzy's father cried. He stared at Tink in wonder. "This is going to be the discovery of the century!"

Vidia saw him raise a glass jar. "Watch out!" she warned. Now that her wings were dry, she was able to fly over and knock Tink out of the way.

SLAM! The jar came down on Vidia instead.

"I must get this to the museum right away!" declared Dr Griffiths.

"Father, you can't do this!" cried Lizzy – but it was no use.

Dr Griffiths ran out of the house, jumped into his car, and drove off to the city. When the other fairies arrived, Tink told them that Vidia was in danger. "We have to hurry and rescue her!" she cried.

It was still raining, though. The fairies wouldn't be able to fly.

"We can't fly," said Tink, "but I think I know somebody who can."

The fairies swirled around Lizzy and showered her with pixie dust.

"All aboard!" cried Tinker Bell.

The fairies tucked themselves into Lizzy's raincoat, and off she flew down the road that led to the city.

Shortly after nightfall, the magnificent streets of London came into view.

"There he is!" cried Lizzy as she spotted her father's car.

Tinker Bell flew down and bravely darted into the engine. After some quick tinkering, the car sputtered and stopped.

Dr Griffiths jumped out and raced off towards the museum on foot. Tinker Bell – and Lizzy – were right behind him.

"Father!" Lizzy called.

Dr Griffiths turned to see his daughter flying toward him. "Lizzy... you're... flying!

"But I don't understand," Dr Griffiths continued.

"You don't have to understand," Lizzy told her father.

Dr Griffiths looked at all the tiny magical fairies hovering around him. His eyes filled with wonder. "I just need to believe," he said. He handed the jar to Lizzy. Seconds later, Vidia was reunited with her relieved and grateful friends.

Then everyone – including Dr Griffiths – received a generous sprinkling of pixie dust and flew back to the country.

The next day, everyone enjoyed a lovely tea party in the meadow.

"Isn't this pleasant, Father?" asked Lizzy.

"I can't imagine anything better," Dr Griffiths answered. "Although flying over London Bridge is a close second."

Tink and Vidia sat together, sipping their tea. Not only did they know each other better now – but they had actually become good friends!

A little while later, everyone settled in to hear Dr Griffiths read from Lizzy's fairy field journal.

Just then, Terence returned from his pixie dust deliveries. "Well," he said to Tinker Bell, "you found something to fix after all."

Tink looked at Lizzy snuggled close to her father.

"I guess I did," she replied with a satisfied smile.

The End

A little while later, everyone settled in to hear Dr Griffiths read from Lizzy's fairy field journal.

Just then, Terence returned from his pixie dust deliveries. "Well," he said to Tinker Bell, "you found something to fix after all."

Tink looked at Lizzy snuggled close to her father. "I guess I did," she replied with a satisfied smile.

The End